My Old Pal, Oscar

by Amy Hest

illustrated by Amy Bates

Abrams Books for Young Readers
New York

THE ILLUSTRATIONS IN THIS BOOK WERE CREATED USING PENCIL AND WATERCOLOR.

Library of Congress Cataloging-in-Publication Data

Hest, Amy.
My old pal, Oscar / words by Amy Hest ; pictures by Amy Bates.
pages cm
Summary: "After a young boy's beloved dog dies, the boy encounters a stray dog on the beach. At first, the boy is not interested in having another dog as a pet, but as he walks and plays on the beach, he gradually becomes interested in taking care of the stray dog as a pet"— Provided by publisher.
ISBN 978-1-4197-1901-1 (alk. paper)
[1. Dogs—Fiction. 2. Death—Fiction.] I. Bates, Amy June, illustrator. II. Title.
PZ7.H4375My 2016
[E]—dc23
2015017028

Text copyright © 2016 Amy Hest
Illustration copyright © 2016 Amy Bates
Book design by Chad W. Beckerman

Printed and bound in China
10 9 8 7 6 5 4 3 2 1

Abrams Books for Young Readers are available at special discounts when purchased in quantity for premiums and promotions as well as fundraising or educational use. Special editions can also be created to specification. For details, contact specialsales@abramsbooks.com or the address below.

ABRAMS
THE ART OF BOOKS SINCE 1949
115 West 18th Street
New York, NY 10011
www.abramsbooks.com

For my good pal, Nancy.
My really good pal.
—A.H.

For Sean, who helped me
with the last picture.
—A.B.

Hello, you. Who *are* you?
No tags? No name?
You sure are little. Except for those feet.
Those four big feet making footprints in the sand.

Well, so long.
Good-bye.
Have a nice day.

What? You again?
All by yourself?
   You and that beard.
That soft puppy beard.

I'm not looking at you.
No sir. No way. Good-bye.

I know what you want. You want to be pals.
Well, we *can't* be pals. No sir. No way.
Won't. Ever. Do. That. Again. Ever.
You know who was my pal? *Oscar.*
My old pal, Oscar. My one and only dog.

So go on, you. You and those big black
eyes, go *on.*

Okay, *fine*. We'll walk on
the beach, if you want.

You know who loved the beach? Oscar. He loved the windy days best, and splashing up the sea. After he died, the very next day, I came to the beach to say good-bye. The waves were really, really big, and I was really, really sad. "I'll never stop missing Oscar," I said. "I'll never stop being sad."

Afterwards, I made a picture of Oscar, and I put it near my bed. "Night, old pal," I whisper every night. And "Hey, old pal," in the morning.

See those clouds? Those are big storm
clouds. Oscar knew about storms. He
knew when they were coming. And always
chased us off the beach, my Oscar. He
ran like the wind, and we ran, too,
away from the storm.

Ka-BAM! Ka-BANG! Ka-BAM!

Uh-oh, thunder!
Better run now!
Better run fast!

What? Me, carry you?
Okay, *fine*. Up you go,
up in my big strong arms,
and we'll run like the
wind, like Oscar.

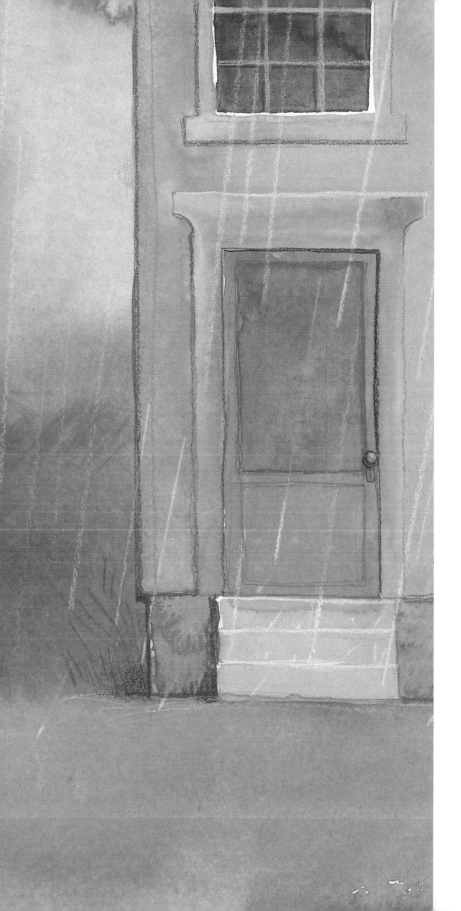

Here's my house. This
little gray house. Come on
in, don't be shy. See? The
storm's out there, and we're
in here. Come on upstairs,
and I'll show you my picture
of Oscar.

Oscar was brave in a storm.
Like me in a storm. Except the loud
ones made him cry. So I put him on
my bed. Which he liked. And tickled
his ear. Which he liked. And under
his chin. And when Oscar was ready,
he yelled at the storm. He yelled and
yelled. And all that yelling made him
really, really sleepy. So he curled up
tight. And slept right through to
the end of the storm.

Hello, you.

No tags. No name. And really, really sleepy.

So, sleep, little pal, and I'll work on your name. You *need* a good name. Sleep right through to the end of the storm, and when you wake up, you'll have a good name, and we'll both be home together.